Irene

The Andromeda

Josephs Quartzy

ISBN 978-93-5610-592-8
© Josephs Quartzy 2022
Published in India 2022 by Pencil

A brand of

One Point Six Technologies Pvt. Ltd.
123, Building J2, Shram Seva Premises,
Wadala Truck Terminal, Wadala (E)
Mumbai 400037, Maharashtra, INDIA
E connect@thepencilapp.com
W www.thepencilapp.com

Author biography

Joseph Marwa (born April 16th, 1999) proffesionally known to as **Josephs Quartzy** is a Tanzanian Singer-songwriter, Actor, Author and Entrepreneur. Josephs is notable by songs; *Coder, I'm a Rider, Dear mama2* and *Promise,* movies; *Mr Local Man (2019), Lucifer'e and the great Controversy (2020)* and a Tv show *JQKnewThat.* As an author, Josephs is writing on a high range of genres, but he is mostly known on writing fictional as well as philosophical novels. He is known for his *I Married a dead woman, The Power of Love* and *A Tale of an Intelligent Psychopath: Based on a true story* books. He serves as the current CEO of Bongo Times.

CONTENTS

Acknowledgements

Almight God is to be tganked before anything or anyone else since he gives me things that not any human can give me, He is unexplainable.

I should thank myself for being me, for trying and accepting the criticism because once I accepted them at first and worked out to correct on whatever I went wrong, I became stronger.

I will not be grateful if I don't give a word in return to these nicest people who were always there when I needed them the most, assisting me with one or two things and have worked hard to make this story readable today.

Irene P.M: This is a special girl who is a fuel to whatever happened into this beautiful story, she is the flower and a good scent in here, I really thank her for all the moment she gave me to collect data for today's use.

Dr. Eliah T.C: My brother, my best friend is always the best man I could trust and like. Thank you very much and continue to be there as you always does.

Partick C.M: I think I could not write books if it were not for you, you are a great inspiration of my writing career, I'll tell everyone in evrybook I write.

Alex J.M: You are a real brother, though money is your priority but you always trust in my capabilities and talets. Thank you too.

Asma S.M: You've got my special thanks as you are very special to me and I wish it to be the same always.

My special Thanks go to Mahende Secondary school's staff, students and a board of directors for trying harder for your students, you gave me the most amazing moments I can never forget.

Introduction

The last time I saw her was the the day I could not talk to her even if I wanted and she would not talk me to even if she wished so badly, she looked as beautiful as a fairy that day but she was very sad in her eyes which were red like she been crying the whole night, her beautiful light face that always smiled seemed red like she was hit by something on her face or she has been sick for months, everyone could notice that, I wanted to approach to her, grab her tightly and ask her who made her cry but all I could do was pretending to be busy with my own activities, I could only watch her walk slowly until she dissappeared from my sight. She wore a tight sized milky gown that day, that went on showing her well structured sexy body she was having, a gown she had received as a graduation gift and a very beautiful high heels pair of shoes. I saw both of those outfits on that same day she was given as gift but I still regret that I never had a chance to tell her how beautiful she looked on them.

****

Here is a true story of the only Andromenda I happened to witness in my life, the love of my life and my first love who had shaken my heart to its core.

Irene an amazing girl that I'll always thank God for making her part of my life, I learned a lot from her and the relationship we had. I was a bit childish with a boyish lifestyle but I would undertand and kept a record of all that happened at that time.

It as been almost three years since I last talked to Irene and about six years since we called an end to that beautiful love we struggled making and keeping for almost four years. Due to broken-heart, anger and frustration I failed to keep as many records of her like pictures, written notes, voice notes, or even a diary I wrote of her, I hardly kept only one piece of paper she sent me at times I was sick back then. It's been almost eight years but I've since kept that precious gift from Irene to all the places I've gone.

I don't clearly remember the last cool conversation I had with her but I clearly remember how beautiful it all started and we both should stick together from the beginning of this beautiful story to see if she deserves to be called an Andromeda or not.

Form one A careless boy

I reported at MHDSTR secondary school on Friday of January 28th, 2013 as the 16th student the school had ever received because our class was their first ever installment contrary to Irene who had reported to school a very long time ago as the second ever student to report to school.

Our school was located in between sorrounding bushes and a light forest, with only wild animals like hyenas, owls and wild rabbits as our only neighbors. One added student was welcomed like a god because he/she would add something that would cover a small part of the school emptiness.

I could not notice Irene at the first sight at school though I saw a number of girls secretly observing a male newcomer and later on would consider Irene was there too though I was never sure a hundred percent about that.

Irene came from a lower-middle class family where her father (Mr. Paul) was a mini truck driver and her mother (Mrs. Paul) was a nurse at a diocese local dispensary so she was not eastimated to earn as much as a nurse from a government hospital but both parents Mr. and Mrs. Paul loved their daughter (Irene) that they would rather starve to send her to a better school even an expensive one. Her parents believed in her and they had probably seen a little genius girl in her.

Irene was a very humble girl, taking alot of her time alone

studying and revising contrary to I, a very busy and stubborn little guy who was busy getting into troubles, playing and fighting because I could feel like I was much different from a large number of students at that school because I was the only one student from a far region, secondly, I had repeated the class so I would see the rest of the classmates as little pickins doing what I've already done and thirdly, I was living like a spoiled dumb child since I came from upper-middle class family where my dad was a very known engeneer and a businessman also one of the richest men of our home village at a time.

One of the first girls I hated from MHDSTR secondary school was Irene because her humbleness was very much like an act but maybe because the students were both aliens to one another so it was bad to act all bad to people you don't know, Irene was actually a very fierce type of a girl and was never good listening to her when you are in a quarrel because they were annoyance and if you are much more capable of her you would end up beating her up adding that she had a very terrible voice, you would even think she is insulting you but she is actually insisting on something.

I remember slapping her once because of her fishy words I never liked, she ended up cursing me the whole year but that was before everything.

****

We were so 'damn' young when we first saw one another because Irene was on the same age as me the time we met, we both were thirteen but I would reach fourteen three months later and she had to wait further five months to reach fourteen.

Irene went on dating the youngest boy of all students

calked Vena as her first school lover boy the same year we attended to school making a record as one of the first relationships at MHDSTR secondary school. All I could remember about her relationship with Vena was that, they always had fights and their ego made it even worse and they dumped one another. I could not bother on going about asking about her relationship statues because she was one of the girls I hated at that time and I could not bother knowing anything about her.

I went on dating a big school gurl and I would make the same record as Irene too though she was too way forward to be in a relationship than me.

The big girl was called Marry, she had a well built figure for a girl of her age, she had a big figure than all girls at MHDSTR secondary school and a well experienced girl in terms of sex than all because I happened to date alot of them.

If I won't take much of your time, I should talk abit about Marry. Marry was there already when I reported at MHDSTR and we went on becoming big friends because I loved jokes and she was a big fan of my jokes, I happened to have a friend called Ally with arab ancestry who was taking me lightly in terms of girls and relationships and was true because I never dated anybody before and I was not going well with girls, I was a troble maker and a short tempered individual plus I was still a kinda, how would I know about relationships or sex?.

Ally wondered on how I would be friends with a girl and nothinv happens, with his terrible english he said, "Josema, how are you making a girl laugh without even approaching her, if she laugh at your jokes daily and she always stay with you, she live you" he kept quiet then added, "that lucky fell to a wrong guy, he is loved but will never understand". I could never understand Ally's words because I was a newbie to those things plus I could think of his as a lier because, how would he know girls thoughts? "No that's a lie, she never loves me" that is what I would reply whenever I would remember Ally's words but as yime went by, Ally's words became much more stronger inside my gead and I could no longer ignore them, I had to take a step forwad so, I approached Ally and asked him on how I should do to get Marry.

Ally was very happy and said, "yo, now you're my man, let's do this" he told me to write a simple letter to Marry asking her to date me and that I fell for her. "Mmh....That was is hardest one, I truly never felt that way and what if she reject my request? I could never imagine how I will be turned a laughingstock at MHDSTR". Ally kept insisting and for the sake of our friendship, I agreed to that and I had taken the risk.

Under a mango tree that's where I submitted the letter to Marry who went on replying me on evening one same paper, after giving her the letter I could not stay put the whole day I would go to toilet to pee every time, I would tremble with no reason at all and between conversations I found myself giving alot of 'off points' repeatedly.

I opened the letter and found only one line written, and the moment she gave me, she did not turn back or even greet me, she gave me and went away and I whispered, " that's what I was talking about, a divorce before damn marriage, I hate this little man, Ally" but Ally foresaw love of Marry and he had only helped me, I realized that after opening the letter and read that one line carrying two sentences, "I agree, I love you too". That was an exciting news but to me that seemed a new problem because I used to stay all alone plus I was a newbie when it came to love affairs and I didn't know what would be the next step after that 'yes', how am I going to face her as my new lover? that was too crazy but thanks to Ally I had all the procedure done.

I could not talk to or came across Marry for more than two weeks since we had so called 'relationship' but one evening during preps time, about 8PM per Ally's influence, I had written a piece of paper to Marry telling her that I wanted to hug her and touch her boobs, I dont know why I wrote that but thanks again to Ally who made me do the unthinkable, she agreed and we agreed that we should request permission to ho out from matron and she allowed us to, I personally asked her permission to have a 'short call' like weeing or just peeing and I was allowed.

I found Marry at the wrong direction, she was just standing outside boys toilets though I had told her to wait for me behind girls toilets on one of the side walls with enough shades, I quickly grabbed her hand and pulled her to the direction because I didn't like to see the next scene after somebody has seen us there.

For the first time in my life I was standing in front of a girl and I was required to take further steps all by myself, Ally was nowhere to tell me what I should do next, It was only me and Marry, that's the day I missed Ally the most. but I had to depend on the nude movies I had watched and adult books I had secretly read to save my 'ass'.

After a quiet moment of two to three minutes, without even thinking I quickly hugged her, and placed my head on her chest because I was so small compared to her large body size that was almost two times bigger compared to my tiny body size, I could feel the warmth of her breasts and her racing heart, All I could do was tightening my hands and squeeze my lips closer and closer to her lips, she hadd touched me too and had me come even more closer the same time we were having a very deep kiss changing saliva, I automatically found my hands touching her breasts at a time I felt her sized 'stand still' breasts with a long nipple that had risen because of sensation she was feeling, I slowly pulled up her t-shirt she was wearing and saw that she had not wore a bra, I closely noticed her beautiful stood breasts, that I quickly placed my left hand on her right boob and started playing with her nipple and rotating my hand around her boob while my mouth was on the nipple of her left boob and sucked it slowly that made her make strange noises and her body would keep on moving on different positions.

After sometimes she could no longer keep it going, she lifted her hand and touched my small d*** that was 'still' all way long and rubbed it gently and then pulled off my trouser's belt, unzipped my trouser and pushed it down, she could then touch my small d*** on her hand and continued rubbing it, I could not hold back and pulled off her skirt and I would wonder how beautifully she was built, she had huge hips and butts, I could hesitate taking her hands off my d*** then I came closer to her and grabbed her closer to me and the rest was a story.

I could not believe that I've had sex with Marry because it all started as simple as a joke but we had it done. I could not hold back telling my friends especially Ally on what happened that day and he would smile and nod his head a s a sign of appreciation.

I went on dating Mary for the whole year and we had taken

our relationship to the next level of being sex predators. I remember once The Headmaster had arranged sitting postures for all of the students in the class and I ended up sitting with Marry and that was too worse because I could meet Marry almost the whole day. Ine morning till evening I would be with her on the same desk in the class, and in preparation times, she was among my group members I had to teach, so she was there too, I was with her starting 7AM in the morning to 11PM in the night. During the class hours, we would be touching our body parts almost the whole day and at night in preps hours, all she would do was to rub my d*** the whole night and I would be touching hers too or we we would agree on meeting somewhere safe at night and had the sweetest sex.

The whole relationship between me and Marry was all about sex and we would never bother about things called love or affection and that was the problem as to why we never lasted too long.

After a sudden break-up that I could not understand till today we continued to be good friends, we chat and she still loves my jokes but I miss her body and sex. Marry went on dating July and other several men till she on fell on hands of our patron who she still dates today.

Form Two Love sparks

On 2014, all of us in our class had advanced to the next class that was form two and we had welcomed new student who would be our junior and our school's second ever installment. That is the year I joined my young brother Frankie too.

On the class level we had entered was an examination class means, we had to take national examination to advance to form three the following year, so most of us expected to take the year very serious and I like the other students didn't think if I would have time for unnecessary things like love affairs, stupid activities or anything that would hinder my studying and performances but I was totally wrong, as far as I can remember, that was the year that shaped me into someone I've never been before and I had tatally forgotten about the coming examinations. Not only me, but the whole class had changed to the same style as mine.As people say 'a funeral to many is a celebration' I did not notice if I was racing off-line and I was playing with my 'goddammit life' because everyone was busy majoring in minors like I was.

The junior class that had come didn't miss little beautiful girls and like many other boys in our class I couldn't miss a chance to try my lucky. Though really I don't like dating village girls per my personal reasons, I fell on hands of a black little girl named Lemmy that was indeed a typical illage girl because she was the only one left unoccupied. I was still shy on seducing that's why I had to look on an easy prey to catch and I indeed was very lucky to even get her. We did not last long because we were never a match and even though she seemed very much calm, kind, with lots of dignity and respect, none of my friends or brothers seemed happy about that couple and I dumped her badly for the reasons she never understood to date but I should admit here, I dumped her because she was never a type of an easy girl to have sex with. I rember calling her on a dark chamber to have a little bit of touches but whenever I touched her she would tremble like she had touched a nakes wire with electrons passing on, the moment I pulled her closer I could hear how her hearbeat raced like a formula one racing, she screamed chanting the words I could remember, "leave me alone", "I don't wanna do this", "please", I could never leave her like that and I had taken further steps to touch her young breasts that's a time she freaked out, jumped out of the place we were, breathing heavily and ran away, from that moment on, she never agreed on coming with me anywhere alone and she told me if I would need any meetings with her, I should make them on daytime. I torelated that for days hoping that she would chance but it went for weeks, months and that was too much for me to bear, guess what happened next? I dumped her right on a daytime because she seemed to enjoy the daytimes and it wasn't too bad to borrow her one daytime.

After I parted from Lemmi I had stayed single for quite sometimes and I found that almost all girls whether at our class or the junior class were occupied and since I had not known about overthrowing a man from a girl I dediced to stay all alone and you can't believe I used to that and I remembered a perpose that brought me to school. The moment I turned a blind eye to stupidity, I found alot of people busy with studies and they had no time for anything apart from studying and surviving at school, I think sometimes if you are a t a bad side and see your friends in it you think everyone is in it but that might be a small group compared to a remaining crowd. The only stuff could entertain them was sports and games, I joined a football team and I was a fresh person, Josema the footballer.

We had done a regional examination on july that year and I had excelled more than almost everyone, I could again defend my position as one of the best students at school.

****

Dramas had started afresh when Elia, my young brother whom we were on the same class loved Irene who was literally my enemy at that time and I was the first person he would ask me to be his delivery boy as he always did, It was very hard for me because I never wanted that job since Irene was my enemy and I was a renowned prefect at our school so it was a little bit of a shame for me to be a delivery boy but for Elia, I would put my ego aside and do whatever I could to assist him because apart from being my brother, Eliah was and still is my best friend whom I can entrust all of my secrets, so I went on doing that work. The job was not very good and was very much annoying because I remember the first day derivering a piece of paper Eliah had sweated writing and I had watched him struggling all night oprning dictionaries looking for nicer words a girl would like but apart from looking me in a bad manner, she wrote a big bold 'no' on Elia's paper, that was really annoying and I blamed alot when I returned a reply to Elia. That evening I swore to talk to her about Elia and what she did. I called her on my table which I was sitting with only my friends and no one apart from my company would dare sit there and that was for everybody with a gang or with any kind of superiority at school.

She responded to my call and we had to talk about that day's incident, I did not have any feelings for her the whole time I talked to her because that was all about Elia and I never looked her with a seductive eye or even intentions of seducing her.

I always though she was a bizarre girl as earlier that day but the moment I went on talking to her I realized that she was very much matured than how people thought of her, infact, she was the most hated person I knew at school and she had fought with a lot of students also she was a girl that had been seduced by almost every boy in my class except me and she denied all except one Vena, who she also dumped few months after a controversial date.

She gave me a really proper reason for dumping Elia and after I had told Elia, he agreed with her and they went on becoming friends, she said, "You know Joe ain't big but I know a thing or two about love, you know I feel Elia but I won't date her, he is a good boy, unfortunately he is not my type, he deserves better, and I don't think If I could ever love him even if I say yes, he better understand that no I wrote".

****

After a long stay at school, the moment everyone was waiting came on, it was a time for the national examination and after that everyone was going home.

"ooh home, sweet home, feel lonely, miss home,went rome, far east, loved one, still wanna, go home, sweet home"

That was the song I could sing every evening at times I was taking shower or fetching water because I had nothing or no one to miss at school and I had missed home like nothing else.

The days for examination approached and we were inside a cold room that would be very hot to anyone who sees hardest questions on his/her questions paper or time has run out he/she has done nothing to satisfy him/herself.

We were doing an examination on ten subjects with no an option to leave any subject and on friday we entered in the examination room to finish the last examination, a bible knowledge examination, since I was very sharp and with high accuracy that some of my friends dared calling me a bible genius. I always finished the first the same as that day, I had finished first and got out of the examination room to wait for my fellow student and pretend to be a marking schemeand was the game for top students.

Fifteen minutes later someone came out of the examination class, I smiled because I gelt like a company was voming for my loneliness rescue, I had expected to be one of my friends but NOPE, Irene was the one coming out of that class, how could possibly be her? I did not like the Idea of her finishing next to me but I couldn't avoid the fact that she was indeed the second to finish the exam and she was the second to come out.

I did not expect her to come at a place I was sitting since

we were never getting along, I expected her to leave that place immediately into her dormitory but guesss what? She came and sat near me just some centimeters away, I really felt uncomfortable that day because I could neither chase nor welcome her, I just sat like a statue, looked focused but my brain was in a great chaos.Irene was the first to start the conversation only two minutes of quietness, she asked me "don't you want me here?" I actually did not want her but she knew I would never chase her, I found myself blabbering words infront of a girl forthe first time in my life, "Nope, I could never do that, maybe you are the one who doesn't want to stay her" woooo!! what was I doing? welcoming her? talking to her like I was apologizing? that was never my style but it came automatically and Irene was very beautiful to just chase her away.

Irene smiled and said "you seem to be a bit troubled, by the way are you well?" Infact she was the one troubling me, I tried to hide my frustrations but I didn't know that the harder I tried to hide them was very much like exposing them.I answered, "nope, it's not about anything, maybe I just feel hungry since I did not take anything since morning and I feel like I'm becoming weak but I'm fine" she interrupted,"cooks have already brought the buns and you're here crying hungry, you should buy some" I felt so much cared that day,and I slowly was dancing to her beats, I added,"mmh!! Okay, I would have done that already but you know they're not given for free and I'm penniless". She laughed very loud and said,"you're lying, isn't?" I quickly answered,"noo, I'm not", she said,"How on earth could the son of a rich man cry for being hungry?, that's insane, how should the rest of us do?". I had enough pocket money to buy buns for all the students in a whole week but I enjoyed the conversations with her and I loved teasing her very much, she knew I was lying and bur she said while waking up, "worry out, just wait for me here, I'm going to look if I still have something in my wallet". I did not believe what I just heard, no one has ever given anything let alone money by a girl in that manner, I just smiled and shouted to her because she had already reached far, "just two hundred will be enough" one bun is sold one hundred Tanzanian shillings, so two hundred shillings would buy two buns, she just nodded her head indicating that she was agreeing to me.

When the short break bell rang I was on the same place making some stories with friends who had come out of an examination room soon but I literally was waiting for Irene to appear and there she was, after a proper waiting, the last one holding her big green cup ready for morning porridge, I could not drink porridge that day like the rest of my classmates simply because that was the day we had to go home because we had nothing to do at school, we had finished the final examination, we only waited to be summoned by the Headmaster and be given a proper farewell but there she was, with a big cup, I could not hold my laughter neither my friends but all of our laughter was stopped when she called me out loud, "hey, Josema vould you please come here?", I felt Abit shy and everyone was shocked because they all knew that I was not going well with Irene and she was the arrogant type of a girl to call anyone, she knew that she was too beautiful than any girl at school so calling a boy out on that manner was like giving him some credits but she did called me, I could hardly notice how people had stopped their work looking at that moment of majic, that was between a beautiful arrogant girl and a rude, spoilt son of a rich man. People wondered as to how would Irene the beautiful chick call Josema, her sworn enemy, and they would wait to see what I was about to react, they though I would freak out and tell her things like "come here yourself" or "no" but they wondered because I slowly walked towards her smiling and saw that she had gave me something and whispered some words to me, running away to the cafeteria, they wanted to cry out loud. Infact I was the one started talking to her telling her how could she call me out there, that was like exposing that we had something going on between us but she told me to let that be because she didn't care, she took three steps forward then turned and said,"make sure you are satisfied, and don't give me change", when I unfolded my hand to see the amount she had given me was a one thousand Tanzanian shillings note," Whaat!! hey you, come back here," I shouted to her exclaimed, but she had no signs of stopping and I remained on the same spot just standing with nothing to do. I slowly walked towards the cafeteria bacause I knew if I had returned to the place I was with my friends who were still on the same spot wondering, I could never answer all of their questions, especially Elia's questions.

I went on buying thirty buns for my friends to eat, because I was not even hungry and I had to do something to calm them down and I seemed very harsh to anyone trying to dig 'gold' inside of me.I kept that one thousand note Irene had given to me, it was like a precious jewelry inside my wallet and when the time had passed since the break had finished, we were summoned to close school, the moment that everyone was waiting but I no longer wanted it because I felt that I had a reason to stay longer at school, by the way that was never going to happen because we had to leave the school.

****

After the announcements from the Headmaster and the school Director we were allowed to ho home untill the following year on the fixed date.Everyone seemed very happy but I was no longer happy with our departure from the school, I know that was because of Irene.

I didn't see Irene for a moment and I thought I would go home without even seeing her or say "thanks for today"as time went by, everyone was going and I was there with Elia waiting for someone who was keeping our mobile phones to come and give them to us. I was told that someone in the cafeteria was calling me, I wanted to ignore that call but since I had nothing to do, I went on to respond a call from that person, she was a cook, my old friend who wanted to borrow me some money with alot of reasons behind that borrowing, I didn't want to hear alot of stuffs that day so I gave her that money thoug I gave her some, not all the amount she requested because I knew she was not telling me the truth and she was not good at paying back her debts. I turned back and started walking away but I had to stop right away because I could not believe whom I was seeing, Irene was right infront of my eyes entering the cafeteria, she was heading to the same cook to borrow a phone to speak to her parents, what a lucky day I was having.

I had told her that she should come and meet me at the dining hall's front chairs I'll be waiting for her with a reason she couldn't refuse that I wanted to thank her properly, she said "okay, I'll be there shortly", I went on sitting down waiting and after sometimes she came and sat there next to me, instead of saying anything I felt my heart beating rapidly and I was breathing heavily because I felt like I was in between a room with no oxygen gas, I could not even talk a single thing after a 'how are you?'. She saw all that but she kept quiet, she only smiled looking at me on my eyes directly, I stated talking much more like stammering, "I must pay you back the money you owe me the next time we come again, I guess I'll have all of your money plus interest, by the way thanks so much I didn't know if you cared about me because of the situations we were in", she interrupted,noo Jose I think that was bot agreed to be a debt, ain't a loans shark, you were cool today and I felt like giving you that", "woo, thanks then" I interrupted, "will you coming back here on to MHDSTR the next year?" I asked, I wondered the same as she wondered, since when did I start caring about somebody's warfare especially a girl?..Was I in love already?. I actually did not want to know, "I like ut here, if God keep blessing my family not to miss school fee I think I must come back".She said. "What about you?" she then added, "aah coming is the must for me" I replied smiling.

After a long time making alot of interesting stories, almost everybody in our class had gone home except for me, Elia, Irene and other two girls but me and Irene were the cause for them to delay simply because Irene was waiting for me because we are brothers and those two girls were simply waiting for Irene to come too.

I lastly asked her the most important thing at a time, her number, "do you have a phone?" I asked, "why would you someone at this age miss a phone?" she replied me with a well elaborated question. "Okay then, Imma gonna need it, if you won't mind","okay" she replied then asked for my palm to write it on, whaaaaaaaaaaaaat!! That was much more than the word awesome, I can't expalin how that felt like, I really felt very great that I even wanted to ask her write all of her relatives phone numbers. I knew she didn't want my number because I thought I might be feeling that way all alone but no she said,"are you that selfish, caring about yourself?" I shockingly asked,"why is that?" I though I might have said do something that had upset her, "do I look like I don't want yours?" she asked, "what If you loose mine, won't it look like I have wasted my precious time?" I could not believe what I just heard, "Irene wants my phone number too?" I never asked out loudl but anyone would know what my question was through my facial expression at that time all in all I quickly looked for her right hand that had embraced herself with and pulled it out and quickly wrote two phone numbers on her palm instead of one telling her that if she could not get me with one between and then I run away because I felt like I had got everything I wanted.

I apologized to Elia for the delay and promised to buy him something he would like, then we started a journey home.

****

I was living very far from the school almost four regions apart that it would take me two days by bus to reach home. I reached home safely where everyone had missed me and I had missed everything and everyone at home aspecially my room.

My phone had shut down because the batter had nonpower so I had to charge it and it was on, you can't believe but I managed to keep Irene's numbers on my palm without erasure, I don't know how I managed to keep them to that far but I actually did.

I successfully copied Irene's number to my phone and saved them, I tried to reach the by sms on the first days but messages were not derivering, I took heed and tried to call her but she was actually unavailable for days that I thought she lied to me and made fun of me for giving me the wrong phone numbers.

The moment I returned back home I found that they had brought a new house maid (Sara) at home whom I made a good friend. She was a very tall beautiful girl, almost four years older me, the only problem she had with, was talking too much that she always annoyed people near her including me but she and I went on to became very close friends since I always helped her with house chores but as time went by she showed all signs of loving me and I could not play with that chance simply because Irene had played me also I felt like having sex, I also needed an experience on these things so I had to dance according to the tunes. Without even seducing her, we went on thinking about sex because we were very horny after a long time without having sex.

My room was next to hers so, at night she came by into my room with an excuse of watching a movie clip from my phone that she liked the thing I could not deny, I understood all she wanted but I was too afraid to start the fire inside the bush. We we lied in a facedown posture to both see well on that small screen though my thoughts were never at that video she was watching repeatedly. At midnight I encouraged myself to start what she wanted. I started by putting my hand on her shoulder and started rubbing her smoothly like I was massaging her shoulder, after a long rubbing in which she only grunted like a pig, I took the most crucial step, I extended my hand to touch one of her breasts and started playing with her nipple, instead of forcing me to leave her, she started moaning with pleasure like she was tickled and suddenly she turned on my side and grabbed my head closer, put her lips on mine and we should call the rest history. I went on doing sex with Sara almost everyday during that holiday that I almost forgot everything about Irene.

One evening when I was watching Television at home with my young brothers who had closed school recently, I reveived a message written "Hi Joe" on a number that I had saved 'The special 1' before and that was Irene's. I could not believe it, that was way too scarry and surprising at once. Though we were not dating, I felt like I had alresdy cheated her so I could not reply herat the same time, though she was four regions away from me, I felt like she was watching all dirty I was doing all along. All in all I went on having sex with Sara even after felt guilty.

In the evening I replied her text with "I thought you gave me a non existent number, I wated too long", she quickly replied,"I had to look for a new phone, mine was broken, so sorry though", "worry not" I replied. We chatted the whole evening until around 7PM when she told me that she had to go cook dinner for the family.

I was staring on my phone waiting for Irene's message when she called,

Her: "hey"

Me: "Hey"

Her:"I'm free now let's chat, though I won't exceed 10PM"
Me: "ok, I'll respect that"
Her: "Temme"
Me: "Missin u"
Her:"thankx"
among the things I hated the most was egoistic people like Irene, for things like deeply telling her you miss her and she reply thanks, that was indeed a great level of abase but I was in need so I had to toil inside that mud of what I thought to be the same as humiliation. so we went on chatting and I already knew that conversation will not go any further, so I replied to her 'thanks'
Me: "ok"
Her: "Enhe"
Me: "What"
Her: "nothing"
Me: "Too here"
Her: "I should sleep now"
Me: "Yah, yo've lot of growth to do"
Her: "Hahaha, me growing up?"
After seeing that I did not show any signs of bringing up any stories, she tried to make an angry man laugh to stupidity, thay would never be me I could never support her laughter gesture I angrily replied off-point.
Me: "Ok, goodnight
Her: "Mh!! Why is that"
Me: (quiet)
Her: "Hey"
Me: (quiet)
Her: "goodnight then"
Me: "Too here" (four hours later at 1 AM)
Like her, I was a good example of an egoistic person

adding the fact that I was still a young boy I could never agree the fact that I tell her I miss her and she does not say me too. I did not understand ways of life yet, I was a man of fire for fire, water for water. We had planned to chat until 10PM that would make two hours but we only had chat for seven minutes that day because of 'thanks'.

I could not find Irene the next days days and since Sara was there, she gave a good reason not to miss Irene. She was a good pretender, she did not find me either. Hours went on, days flew, we were now on a new year without hearing anything from one another.

Form Three Love & Betrayal

A new year had come, 2015 a really cool year we were eagerly waiting because we were entering the next class that was form three.The results came out they were all over the enternet, since I had a smartphone I could look them easily. The whole of our class had passed the exam, I got a division one with an average of a GPA of 4.9 and Irene had a GPA of 4.7, the highest of all girls. She was among the brightness female students I ever studied with.

I was on the preparations week because we soon were opening the school again, I could not delay as I always did since the class we were entering was the toughest of all and I had to be a little serious about it. Everyone was very happy because we were opening the school again except for me and maybe for some ather few students. I neither did not want to leave free sex from Sara, nice foods nor using my expensive smartphone but that choice was never mine to make, I had to leave home when the school opens. I thought Irene will never be my type because of ego driving her without even turning back qnd look at ego that was driving me crazy, I lived per people's stories concerning Irene and I was too young to know things and since she never texted me I could never do it either and that was all.

Only five days to opening day, the number I saved 'The special one' texted me "I miss you", I started trembling after I had looked at that text because I did not want to reply to a sender but the feelings I felt at that time made me stuck in between 'answer' and 'don't answer' options with trembling as the only constant option. Irene knew what she had done all way and that was her style of seeking forgiveness expecting me to calm myself down by avenging her with 'thanks' as she did first but I kept quiet until I was calm to even think of replying her. I took my phone to reply her after sometimes, I found that she had sent alot of texts I didn't hear because I left her chatting space opened all long, I had prepared a very good answer to give her but I could never believe my eyes when I read texts sent by this arrogant girl, she wrote alot of messages in a sequence; "hey", "hey you", "Joe", "so you can't reply", "reply before I get angry", "by the way I wanted to ask you about school and not otherwise", "I regret wasting my money adding creding calling you", "You think you're special?,NOPE, ask anyone and they will tell you the real you". I laughed very loud because Irene was one of the special people indeed, so, was she insulting me bacause I delayed to reply her back? I wrote one of the longest essays I ever wrote, full of insults, abuses, and every kind of abase that I made sure that if she read them she would collapse and die of heart attack I quickly sent that essay and quickly turned my phone and took my sim card out of my phone because I never wanted to argue with girls like Irene with full of abusive words.

I went offline for the sedt of the day until the next day when I switched on my phone to find that the message did not reach Irene because It was not an SMS mesage, because of it's length it had changed into an MMS and failed, below that unsent text, Irene had sent quite alot of messages all of them were of seeking forgiveness insisting that she did not send those insukts intentionally, she simply was very angry that I kept quiet all those days without even texting her and even when she texted me, I did not reply her so she got amgry and insulted me hoping that I would reply but I kept quiet too and switched off my phone. I was very cruel to someone who declared a war to me but very weak to someone seeking forgiveness from me orin need of me. I reallg felt guilty that day because I was the centre of everything and I had to reply her now.

Me: "Miss you, superstar"

Her: (quiet)Me: "Had no credits yesterday and switched off ma phone cuz if I had continued looking at yo messages, I would steal to reply ya"

Her: (quiet)

Me: "reply me any year you wish darlin"

She never replied me at that time and for the first time ever I did not get angry for someone I sent a couple of messages without a reply.

She replied to allbof my texts in the late evening and I had to text her back too because I no longer wanted to play with a coin in the toilet I decided to call her and these were our conversation

Me: "Hi"

Her: "Ya"

Me: "Miss you superstart"

Her: "Mic u 2 Joe"

Me: "Didn't expect that "

Her: "What" (pretending like she didn't understand what I was talking about).

Me: "nothin"

Her: "You coming late to school as always? Cuz I don't

expect to see ya at school on sunday"

Me: "I won't delay for you this time"

Her: "For me? Since when"

Me: "dunno but I will"

Her: "hahahh okay, bring me something then"

Me": "Like what"

Her: "anything"

Me: "Okay, hope you gonna bring me anything too"

Her: "I don't have money enough to bring you anything you know me"

Me: "You once saved me from starvation what is that defined that you don't have something that can satisfy me?"

Her: "I borrowed it and I'm still in debt"

Me: "What?"

Her: "Yah"

Me: "Don't do that again cuz I feel like I'm in debt too"

her: "Why can't I do for people I love? I can do it over and over again"

Me: "Love?"

Her: "Yeah but it looks like I should have used like instead"

Me: "It's alright by the way I love you"

Her: (quiet)

Me "What's happening"

her: "Thanks"

Me: "I didn't finish that sentence, I love you but I hate thanks replies you better keep quiet"

Her: "Okay I'm quiet"

Me: "got somethin to tell ya, should I"

Her: "I should go to cook it's almost late, tell me later"

Me: "ok, bye, find me when you're free:

Her: "ok"

I nearly spit everything without even the second though, thank God she gave me sometimes to think though she seemed like she knew what I was about to speak and she was not ready to hear it that's why she stopped me on the way with an excuse I could not deny stopping.

I felt nervous for starting something I didn't know how to keep it going but after a long thought whether I tell her or not, I only remained with the same option of telling her and I only was waiting for her to find me so that I could tell her how I felt and she "checked" me at night and here we were;

Her: "Hey"

Me: "I really hate your hey, can you use another word, please?"

Her: "Hahaha, and stop calling me a superstar then"

Me: "deal"

Her: "deal"

Me: (quiet)

Her: "you're quiet, atleast you should tell me what you wanted to tell me then"

I intended to spit everything the moment I had the chance but when that chance appeared, I suddenly became mute, I didn't know what to say because I feared speaking love things to any girl especially to a girl like Irene whom I loved deeply all in all I had taken off clothes infront of water, I had to bathe, so I tried to give myself courage and continued the chatting;

Me: :"I love you Irene, that's what I wanted to yell you"

Her: "Thanks I like you too"

Me: "I don't mean that liking, I want you to be my best girl" (the word best girl was a fit to simplify the world lover for a shy person like me)

Her: "What do best girls do, cuz I hear they're bridegroom's close friends, are you about to marry?"

Me: "Nope, okay, let me be clear, I'm in love with you, romantically, I mean I really wish you to become something like lover or I should say my woman"

Her: (Laughter)

Me: "Is that funny? I'm so damn serious"

Her: "You're so funny Joe"

Me: "Why so"

Her: "You still don't understand what loving and relationships mean, don't say you love a person that easily, so I'll go with nope"

I felt like I was all naked in the marketplace at daytime, that was so, so heartbreaking and embarrassing, I thought as to why she would use those harsh and direct words to deny me, I was speechless but I had to finish what I started.

Me: "I don't undertand either and I don't know why I'm telling you this but that's how I felt like telling you all this time"

Her: "since when?"

me: "that day that we were all alone, I felt so safety, loved and cared and I've seen you in my dreams since then, I though I may be in love with you and I'm serious"

Her: "Mmh"

Me: "I know you want to deny me at this very point but atleast I've told you what it really felt like from that day but I would be happy if you give me chance to prove what I've just said."

Irene: "what if you're lying, because don't forget that you always don't take things seriously and what if you want to test me like the rest of you? I guess I'll still go with no because all of the options I'm given falls to negative"

Me: "What if all I'm saying comes from my heart, does betraying a brother who once loved you a joke or not a serious thing?"

Her: You might be serious Joe but I never thought of having a lover this early, what if we wait until we reach form four"

Me: "That will be the biggest lie if I tell you I can postpone my love untill next year, that will not be love but something else, I feel like loving you yoday and I always wanted to be near you, I can't imagine any waiting can do to me"

Her: "you seem to be very serious, let's talk tomorrow, I'll think about it too, bye"

She hanged and switched off her phone that I did not have a chance to say anything further to her. The moment I confessed my love for her, it ignited even more and more that I could not sleep at night and that was among the longest nights of my life, even Sara could not touch me from that day because I did not want to hear any voice apart from Irene, I did not anyone to tell me anything concering love apart from Irene and I was very more like a selfish man.

Since I could not sleep that night, I had to pay back that lost sleep so that morning was my body's midnight because I slept untill 11AM and the first thing to do was to look at my phone to see if Irene had texted me or tried to call me, I literally did not expect to see them because of her ego but I hoped so. "Jesu…!" I exclaimed when I witnessed that Irene had tried to call me but I did not picked up my phone and she had also tried to text me two hours ago without a response, "poor me, what is this bad lucky calling me over" I whispered to myself. I quickly wrapped myself up and without a smsecond thought I ran to the bathroom leaning my mouth and washed my face because bathing in the morning has never been in my routine. I did not even ask for breakfast even though I was very hungry since I had skipped dinner talkingwith Irene, I went on to respond all of Irene's texts. I started with telling her the truth that I was still on bed, she had to forgive me that I did not know if she could reach me at that hour then I went on replying her texts which were short but very rufficult questions to answer, she asked; "you said you love me, why?", "What did you love on me?", "How sure can I be that you love me?", "What if I tell you I'm in a relationship?". The first three questions were really difficult to answer and the last question was rather a heartbreaking explanation with a question mark that made me hesitate to answer her questions but I had to do it whether I wanted or no. I wrote; "I said I love you because my heart told me so, I don't think I have any other reason also I didn't love anything of you, I loved you as Irene and I don't think If I can have proof to love you if I'm not given a chance to proof, give a chance and let's see If I love you or not".

I had to reply her on answers coming from my heart because I never wanted to tell her anything about her beauty, sexy body or anything attractive she is having, all I wanted was love and not her body. I knew I dumping was the following step because of the reasons I had provided but Irene was never a moderate girl, she was amazing and I didn't have to be a deceiving fox to live with a fox, all I haf to tell her was truth and I was saved by that truth.

She told me to call her and I didn't hesitate and this was the conversation;

Her: "Hi"

Me: "how do you do"

her: "Fine"

me: "I love you, Irene"

Her: "You were too slow to love me, I loved you since last year, bad of you"

Me: "Loving me, how?"

Her: "You can't believe this but I've loved you since the time you were coming to make up things for Elia but you were pretending as If you knew what the real enemity was like"

Me: "You're lying, you have never said hi to me, how was that loving, I thought you hated me the most and since you're school's most beautiful girl that every boy there wanted to have, you had no time to thing about me"

Her: "(Laughing) I thought about something over a year because you once insulted me that I was never beautiful I should stop that ego telling me that and almost all of the boys would turn back to look at me whenever I passed and would sometimes give me compliments but you never did, I hated you at first but the moment I kept on thinking of you for months I started seeing a your second world you were living in, you were so cool pretending to be the most fierce boy around, you cared everyone whether you knew them or not, you were coming from q rich family but instead of living a luxury life like your brothers, you lived your life like a poor guy, you cared nothing and anyone, but what you believed for"

Me: "I didn't know that, but I don't see those things as good as you put them to be, they make me look more

selfish than what I thought to be"
Her: "Ok"
Me: "so I'm kind of a selfish nigger?"
Her: "Didn't you request something? that ok is the answer".

I did not believe the power of truth at first but from that day one, I would use it to redeem myself whenever I felt like I was going to drown, I did not believe if I was going to be a boyfriend of the most beautiful girl at school, (Irene), that was awesome and that's the moment that made me write something today. I can't explain how she sounded very sweet that day.

We went on chatting as a newly loving couple on all of the following days, she was very sweet too on the coming days and I would skip my meals because I was wahing long chats with her. I felt like telling any of my school friends that I'm in love with Irene but all of them had tried to seduce her and she denied them, I couldn't bear make all of my classmates my enemies because of Irene, what about Elia the closest friend and a brother? No! I can't do it either, he once loved her, what would he think of me if he hears all that? I was very sad because I could never allow anyone to know any kind of relationship going on between me and Irene.

The opening day reached, a sunday that I and Irene were always talking about because we were going to see one another in a different eye, as lovers. I really wanted to go early at school but as days approached to that sunday, I was getting much more nervous, I did not go to school that day giving my parents alot of possible reasons until Tuesday, when the Headmaster called my father and telling him I should be at school at the the same opening week to avoid any severe punishments so I had nowhere to hide.

****I arrived to school on Wednesday and found out that I and Frank, my young brother were the second last students to arrive at school and our punishment was there waiting for us, the next morning, I saw Irene at the morning parade, she was glowing with her beauty that I felt like I couldn't breath properly, and when she turned and looked at me, she killed me with only one eye brink and a smile, ooh! That was awesome. With Irene's presence at school, I could see a very beautiful zero coming for me at the highest speed. The Headmaster came too in that morning assembly and after endless announcements and threats, we tge late comers were allocated to our respective punishment places. I couldn't believe seeing Irene too taking a slasher as me going to do punishment, I wondered how she insisted me on coming early to school on that Sunday but ended up coming the same day as me, and infact she was that last person to arrive at school, she was a real deceiving fox among humans.

At a time we were slashing, I almost got a chance to talk to her but I was very shy to even open my mouth to say anything concering love matters, I saw that spirit in her too, though we were so close to one another no one would dare talk to the other, I spent the whole week of punishment talking to Frank my young brother and few of my classmates but I avoided talking to Irene.

We started attending the classes on the following week in which we were congratulated too for our good performances on the form two National Examination, we now had got used to school life and the normal routine had to go on as before.

I didn't believe that almost two months at school had passed without communicating to Irene in any form let alone meeting, I avoided her the same as she avoided me, analysing the provlem now, I think we each were afraid of one another and our ego was our worst enemy. The first mid-term break had approached and we all went back home, that's when I pretended like I knew talking to her, we would chat like the real pros, chats filled with the word "Love" without putting it into action.

We promised one another that the following term at school we had to establish our telationship for everyone at school to know ans see because I was afraid that Irene could be taken by someone else if I continue being stupid and hide, and here we were at school once again to show what we are made of but the thing was as always, no talking to one another, egoistic love and shyness.

But there happened to come a moment of miracle, our school was invited on the union of secondary schools' sports and games an event that had to run the whole week, each of the students even the teachers were very happy because we atleast had a short vreak to refresh our minds, entertain and have friends from different school, that event has always been cherished by stydent in our country, I too really like it, the good thing about the event is that, not only the players and performers are supposed to go but also teachers and all the school staff members.

I sat on one of the back seats of our school's mini bus attending to the first day of the event, I was with Elia and some other student at the back seat the time where Irene came late and hot all seats occupied, Elia asked him to seat on his thigh because she could get dizzy if she would keep on standing, she had no any other options than sitting on his thighs, I could see how happy Elia was because to him that was more than yes he expected from her, he could turn on my side and brink an eye showing me to witness that, poor Elia, he did not know what was going on netween me and her crush. Elia could not hide anything from me starting from his troubles, life and anything like that and I could not hide anything from him because we were very much more than brothers, we were the best friends even today but when it came the matter of Irene, how could I tell him, love can disintegrate even the most stable relationship, I knew all that, sometimes I could not sleep the whole night because of that sort of thought, at times Elia would come very happy simply he met Irene and she asked him something, to Irene he eas her brother in law, tjough she did not say anything, to Elia she was Irene her crush, how would I make him understand that I went doing things on his back and betrayed him? On his crush? I decided to keep quiet because I could never imagine what would happen if he gets to know it.

****

We arrived at the event ground and it was so beautiful, thousands of students with different uniforms had gathered there cheering up and enjoying, I could see alot of events going on amready because peope could not wait for anyone.

I was among the schools' representative on gootball though I only played for twenty minutes and the game was over, I remember how badly we were thrashed 6-0, though that was very fortunate because they could even thrash us thirty goals. Irene was representing our school on netball.

Our school had only two games to participate in, the girls trolled us alot for putting our school jnto shame but they were nowhere to be found after they were humiliated, beaten 85 points to only 13 points

During the day I got a word from one of our juniors that Irene was looking for me, I couldn't believe it, Irene looking for me? I was very shocked at the same time excited because the news were brought at a time I was with Elia and I was happy because that was the first ever call from Irene, all in all I had to go and hear her out. Elia would follow me behind because he thought he's got a clear chance of talking and seeing Irene but I prayed for Irene not to do anything stupid infront of Elia.

We followed that junior girl Irene had sent to call me and the moment I reached there she only said one sentence, "I'm hungry". That sentence imprisoned me into Elia's cell of explanations because I knoe he would ask, since when did I and Irene got into that stage? Was I and Irene not enemies? Am I contacting Irene behind his back? I felt so small that day but I had to take courage and move on. I went on buying Irene and his crew drinks and we ate simole food at a time we were waiting for school's meal to arrive.

We walked back to school that evening because the school bus had gone to send home the day scholars, I did jot want to talk to anyone on the way because I felt so bad and I asked myself on how I could face Elia on the situation like today but Elia is the man that I've failed to understand to date. He never got angry that day, instead he called Irene and brought her to where I was all alone walking to school, pretended to be busy with someone else and left us there to talk.

"Hi" Irene greeted me first"Hi" I replied witha a sad voice"Don't you want my company? It seems like I bothered you so much today, Was I a nuisance?" she asked"Why did you do that?" I asked without bothering myself answering to her question"what did I do today?" she asked too"spitting all of our relationship to Elia's mind, I didn't like it today, that was a foolish idea" I said sounding angrily"okay" she replied and went ahead of me taking quick and large steps to avoid me.

I could not stop her because I was not cool about her Idea of showing off like that, when I think of tjose days, I consider myself stupid because I wanted to make it open why was I angry? I wanted to hide it too, how long would I hide? I confused very much but I knew I was making a a mistake to solve a mistake and barking to Irene was a mistake, I had to seek her forgiveness before she changes her mind. I run very quick to find her walking very fast on the same speed as she had passed past me, she had a vry serious face looking down that I was even afraid talking to her but I had to talk to her, after all I was a man she was a girl, I was supposed to take the step first.

"I didn't do it purposely, I was blinded by stupid goddammit angry" I said in a low voice "I never wanted Elia to know what was going on between us because you're his crush and you know our relationship…" I added stopping on the way. She did not say a thing, instead she turned her head up and breathed heavily. "will you forgive me?" I asked curiously after seeing her sighing. "Yeah, forgive me too" she said, "I don't have anything to forgive because I was not wronged by anyone today let alone you and Elia whom I wronged, I hope you are going to forgive me" I explained witha happy voice this time because I believed I was already forgiven. After that day's conversation, we decided not to hide like thieves, and to show our love to all even when the teachers knew what was going on between us and that was the worst decision because I soon was going to suffer the great resistance and obstacles from the students who had fallen in love with Irene.

I told the whole truth to Elia on all that happened between me and Irene and infact, Elia is a man of velour as they refer him, he undersmstood me and buried his feelings within his heart and started calling Irene sister in law, he then saw a young girl calked Rachel, who had shifted to our school recently and fell for her, she had a sparrow voice that would make anyone listed to her whenever she sings or talk, shw e was a beautiful one that she attracted almost everyone, it was my duty to pay for my sins and make her Elia's the work that I didn't take long to do and I felt thatmy sins were all cleared, I would date Irene openly and freely from that day on.

We had alot of newcomers at our class, several new students had come to our school to study, I remember four boys and a girl whom I never liked to date because they made my life miserable at school and they were never my friends because of their filthy behaviours. I remember few of them, Agrey was one of them and my desk mate actually who was living his whole life smoking weed, another one called Masi whom I used to call 'pumpkin' because of his big head and a big body but childish mentality was a very egoistic person who fought and cheated to be the greatest at school to unimportant terms but would eventually became the last one at school on every test, this man always majored in minors, he was my choir colleague, another one called Dennis was coming from a nearby town and always called us the village boys and girls because we were there first at our school which was in the bushes and the last one with the same name as mine one was a cool a smooth pebble on the river bank which would be moved by the moving waters, sadly waters which could move him were his filthy friends and the last one had a first name like mine, Joe T. A calm handsome man with big eyes which gave him alot of good nicknames. I retired from school's students government as a dormitory prefect serving a s a general environmental prefect to give chance for new students to try their lucky, Irene contested to be a head girl and she was one, my young brother, Frank was a food prefect, Elia was a time keeper and our class monitor, so all of my closest people were something, I had no chance to waste going about crying for leadership but, among the winners was Masi, 'The pumpkin' who was my successor as the dormitory prefect, whe position which was the mightiest among all the ppsitions at school because a dormintory prefect could even chase school's head boy away from dormitory compounds if it's not a dormitory classes, like I, he was allowed to take the dormitory keys with him all the times. Masi never had that chance froma ny of the schools he studied, so he made himself a small god who hated me the most with no a proper reason at all. If I had decided to contest to keep that position, he would lost badly by getting the maximum of only four votes out of all the votes at school because he was never loved and I had students first on everything that's why they loved me, all in all it was his turn now I had to rest.

I loved the love triangles at school but they actually made

things awesome and lastly, the were very worse to swallow for everyone. I had two young brothers, Elia and Frank who was a junior, Elia was a class monitor and a timekeeper who had a girlfriend, Rachel. Frank was a food prefect who dated headboy's sister, called Dianna, head boy was dating my ex-girlfriend called Marry and I was dating Irene, who was a head girl at a time and I was a retired loved small guy who would like to talk and laugh most of his time.

****

When time flew by I forgot myself and started cheating on Irene by dating other fresh junior girls, I remember dating one of the director's daughter called Sarah, a sister to one of my old true friends called Gideon, he got angry and from that moment on he never wanted to be my friend again I could not understand him because he dated several girls at school but always wanted her sister not to date anyone there, that was too bad but I kept dating her until things went bad to me that I could not ho on dating her any longer, I then fell for another beauty whom I only wanted to have sex with but I ened up remembering Irene and I avoided that. One moment, as a result of an argument whether I could date the most quiet girl at school or not, I found myself on the big trouble because I approached a girl and she agreed but I didn't know that she broke up with Dennis whom they were having a secret relationship, ooh poor me, "why am I making things bad for myself?"
A confusion had come around me which made me drop from my actual performances and teachers would call me

to ask what was happening to me and I would lie alot about it but it was all because the newcomers tried to steal my Irene, I couldn't believe I was now fighting for love instead of what my cruel parent has sent me.

Each one of them tried to seduce Irene with new swagg but they all failed, all they could do was asking how did I get her? When they failed to get the answers they wanted, they came together with a perfect way to get Irene, thry no longer even wanted her, they only wanted to show me that I was never a god.

Who are these 'they'? These were newcomers I hated and few individuals I made them upset, the first was the head boy himself who hated the fact that Frank, my young brother was dating her sister, another one was Giddy whom I dated her sister, another one was Dennis whom I accidentally seduced her girlfriend whom I actually dumped the moment I won a bet, then Masi who was my sworn enemy and they had people with likes of Agrey who was dumped by Irene. I really was in a real life trouble and I knew the truth that I would never get to win over them, all I had to do was crying all alone and I asked God to keep my Irene because I had done all those silly stuffs without thinking properly and that was the truth.

The gang went on having several attempts before getting Irene into their trap, they told her all cheating I had been doing begind her back and they brought evidences, imagine my once closest friend, Gideon going to Irene that I dated her little sister, that was very bad and all they wished for, came true. I was badly dumped by Irene with piece of paper that kept me on bed for weeks.

Irene decided to part her ways with me despite all the excuses I would bring and since it was near the end of the year I thought to have the longest break at home that I would refresh my mind bedore facing angry Irene again.

The time of examinations came and I was all alone in my heart something that I could not hide from the outside, anyone would notice that I was not fine and since the story of me 'dumped' was all over the school because my haters would go on creating a trendy story to defame me and they really hit the point, I was very hurt both inside and outside with nothibg to do at all. I really hated them and I had no achance of making any of them my friends in this life. I wanted to be left alone the whole day, I wanted to study alone and I went to bed early but when the results came out I didn't believe that, for the first time I was the first in our class, I used to be the second third, fourth and I once become the sixth as the lowest position in my secondary life on that year's first term examinations but I didn't get a chance to celebrate that moment.

We closed the school and we headed back home to prepare for our last year at schoom that was eventually the critical one because that year would determine your four spent years at scho and would position you to go on advanced school or that was your end, there was no turning back on the following year.

****

I returned back home safely but very unsafe within, Irene had made my break worse than ever, I looked for any possible ways not to miss her but I failed, thus I decided to use the only possible way, being a playboy. I went on seducing and having sex with a large number of girls expecting that I would forget all I went through but it all was a waste, I missed her day and night but I wouldn't dare looking for her because she dumped me first and she refused my sincere apology and she never looked for me too. I was very sad but that was life and I had to go on with it.

I ended up having sex with Sara like animals, I would go on having her on bed even four times per day, everyday until we were celebrating the new year's eve.

Form Four Breakup

I reported school late as I always did and this time around, I went too far, I skipped the whole month. I didn't have the clear reason for my delay which I could make them as an excuse but I did had one, unofficial but very special, I was dumped by Irene, and this was the reason as to why I never wanted to come to school early. People would have mocked me because I was very much proud of myself since I had a girl that nobody else dared to have and I felt like I lived in heaven, not this time, I was living in a true mental hell thtlat thinking of shifting rhe school.

Irene looked very sad on her eyes, she looked very much likel a sick person and she dailly walked all alone passing through school's roads, she was late for almost everything and soon she stepped down as a head girl, she was not the same Irene who smiled even if she was angry, this time around Irene was a very serious lady looked disturbed inside and outside. I was the same too, I walked along school roads all alone looking down unusual me, contrary Irene, I never walked alone, I usually had a big company of my sworn friend and juniors who were there anywhere I went. Despite the company I could not talk all along the way I went along talking to myself like a mad person, and the whole school saw what was going on between me and Irene, they saw a world of emptiness, a worl of broken love and a world of missing but no one would step up to make it for us because majority of boys wished to have Irene and most of the girls always had wished to date me because of some factors, so me and Irene not dating was a very beautiful moment for them.

I always saw smiles to haters faces especially of those schemed the whole thing of me cheating and I did not like the Idea of them talking about me in allegories, I had started having bad dreams of fighting and quarreling and I was in a state of mental stress that I hated those days to date but I still had to keep on moving because Irene's love wasn't a grim reaper so closing my eyes and ears to continue living was my priority.

Elia had to do one of the great works that no one ever dared to do, he stepped up to have me and Irene back together, it was a very hard decision that if I was in his position I could never even think about doing it but he actually stepped in, talked to Irene first who threw all the blames to me and he came to talk to me and I clear remeber how it went on;

Elia: "Man"

Me: "Man"

Elia: "It's been a week since you last bathed, I talked to Irene about this, she's waiting for you in the dining hall maybe you can listen to her when she tells you to bathe"

The moment I heard Irene's name, my heart blasted like a blasted WWII grenade and my heart started racing like I was on 10 kilometers run, I could not talk a thing than staring at this sweet talker's face, he was a man of understanding people's true feelings and loved to see people all together, he had a quote he loved the most, stating that, 'happiness begins with a smile' a quote that I didn't even liked but he was very correct.

Elia was a very quiet man who always smiled he was a man with alot of fun jokes to not only his friends but anyone else, but he had a weakness too,he was very easy to get angry, very small obstacles would make him frustrated and he was a man who would never listen to advices untill he 'touched the fire' himself.

After a quiet minute, I answered to Elia, pretending like I didn't understand what he was trying to talk about;

Me: "What are you talking about? I don't understand a thing"

Elia: "She's waiting for you man, I don't wanna see you two die of heartbreaking"

Me: "I've moved on man, I don't even need her like she doesn't want me"

Elia: "(laughed)Yeah man I know you've moved and everyone knows you've moved backwards, so stop being stubborn and let's go"

Me: "What are these jokes man, tell her to go"

All those I time I didn't believe that Elia was serious and was talking the truth because I always encountered these types of jokes but 'wait', Elia would never do that to me,

Me: "Hey man, where did you say she is?" I shouted

Elia: "In the DH", wanna go?"

Me: "Let's go see her together"

Elia: "Fine, let me take on my sweater first"

Me: "I'll be waiting for you outside"

After a minute or two he came out of the dormitory where he found me and we were heading to the dining hall where Elia said that Irene was in, I couldn't believe that I was looking Irene the same moment as she was looking in the eyes, I really felt much guilty, I could see all of my mistakes in her beautiful eyes, that moment I felf like I was never correct and I should be on my knees at that time but ego was there for me, I could never do that.

We walked towards the table Irene was sitting and she welcomed us warmly, pretending as if nothing has happened before though for a person like me who was always very close to her, I could clearly see her face in her saddest state.

Irene: "Hi Joe"

Me: "Are you fine?"

Elia: "We are not fine"

Irene laughed

Me: "I am fine, not is for this squirrel in form of elia"

Elia: "Yeah I'm not fine because you are fine negative and I want my fine positive bro back"

Irene smile looking at Elia whom I was looking too

Elia: "I enjoy the thing that you guys love watching but ain't a damn television so take off your ugly eyes off me"

I laughed alot to Elia's jokes since I enjoyed looking at Irene in her happiness moments, even though I knew Elia was doing all these for me and Irene, I did nothing or walked away, he was there to make us look better and believe that we could make it up again and that was a way he thought would make us talk to one another, he knew we missed and loved one another and he took responsibilities because he was there since the beginning. I know this man because I was his closest person at school and home.

Elia pretended like he was never the oart of the story and walked away to the back tables where his young girlfriend, Rachel was sitting, oh no they schemed thus together? I couldn't believe but I was happy since I had a chance to talk to Irene.

Me: "Hi"
Irene: "We've had that already"
Me: "I know but that was under Elia's influence"
Irene: "But that…….."
Me: "You never changed, youre the same, a bold one who would never put her hands up" I interrupted her sentence
Irene: "Thanks to you master hearing that I'm improving on your subject"
Me: " I miss you though"
Irene: "Well, I don't"
Me: "I know"
Irene: "I was lying, don't cry"
Me: "Hahah, should I cry?"
Irene: "You've never cried, you can't"
Me: "I was seeing you everywhere I was hoing, I heard you're name everywhere and I would smell your scent in each of something I touched, I tried hard to forget you because I never knew if I would ever get this chance but my memories scolded me, I remained a walking corpse"
Irene: "What's that for?"
Me: "It's for confession, I love you Irene, Elia saw that and I can see him helping me to get here, I'm not here as that same boy uou used to know but I'm here as a new one whom you never dated and wishes to ask for your heart to keep it safe"
Irene: "You've improved alot, I wonder why you trapped them"
Me: "I said I'm not here as that someone you know, I'm knew please, I know you can't forgive me in that situation but I'm trying to be new if I can correct whatever I had done, I'm regretting so much"
Irene: "I don't want the new anybody and I won't date

anyone new, I only want my old Joe back, if you're new my answer is no, I love somebody else"

Irene had started crying after she had said that sentence angrily, I whispered the words that I couldn't even hear, I wanted to calm her down and wipe tears off her face at the same time I wanted to tell her I'm sorry and I don't want to see her cry but my heart won over my brain and it's thoughts, I found myself close to her hugging her and saying all those thoughts loudly.

We really made a talked scene that day, the watcher really enjoyed the show and tgat was a trendy for months at school.

****

'True love never fade' one of the singers I adore put that sentence into one of her songs and that sentence defined my love for Irene. We went back on track and this time around, haters saw the real fire because neither I or Irene vould listen to their stupid fantasies and false sentiments we knew that none wished good of us and none would replace our broken hearts.

On a graduation day that was around october, I was in a beautiful black suit like anyboy who was graduating except my tie, I wore a skinny necktie while everyone else had a bowtie. I had a very special day prepared by my parents since I got a huge escorted of two cars from home and I had quite alot of relatives coming to congratulate me, I saw Irene who was very beautiful too in a black short skirt matched with a white shirt and a bowtie then a tight waistcoat with a red flower on herleft came up to complete her beautiful graduation dress.

I introduced Irene to everyone of my family member and told them if we happen to be together after sometimes I must marry her, everyone laughed after seeing how much I was blinded by Irene's love but they loved her eventually. I went on having alot of graduation pictures on my camera, I remember taking pictures of, Me with Irene, Elia and a friend called Joe T who came to make my life a living hell, later on.

We took time to enjoy that day's scenery and we were allowed to wear any kind of home's costumes whenever we wished that day and when I called Irene I saw a beautiful angel infront of me wearing a milky gown and very beautiful pairs of high heels shoes, she really looked beautiful that day, that I stacked for a minute or two staring at her.

We went on loving each other sincerely, through sweet and bitter moments besince haters would never let us be, I remember one moment they went on calling Irene a sait-like harlot, a name I never liked they didn't stop there, they went on reporting us to the Headmaster and since they knew the whereabouts of Irene, she was caught red handed and this time around they provoked me to see the response, if I would take the accusations serious or not instead they saw no response but deep inside I kept them still, I never let them go though I had to remain silent to keep my love on.

A hating group came with a perfect choice for me and Irene, they used their friend called Joe T. a handsome and humble man to make their dream come true, they aimed to break that relationship we hardly built out of track and here they were. I was not so close to Joe T but he was my friend to because he never made someone angry and he was very humble whenever he had done something wrong, he would keep quiet and ignore if someone had wringed him, he was a man whom everyone wished to befriend.

I can never hate or blame Joe T. to date because he did all those dirt works for his friends who only manipulated him and got hold of his good status and respect at school, he could not deny any of their orders because they were his friends, they were the most powerful gang at school and they were always doing things in cooperation. Joe T had joined them for only school's daily survival but this time around, he had to cooperate in breaking someone's love and he was in it.

The gang used Joe T to seduce Irene to get my attention and see what would happen next, Irene had managed to deny Joe T at first but she went on seeing him everyday that she could not deny him but she neither agreed on his requests. The time went on and we were only remained with 30 days before finishing our ordinary secondary school level at MHDSTR, they wanted to make things fast so that I cry before going home and thus, they came up with a perfect way to trap me.

Since Joe T and Irene wouls spend alot of time together, they started making strong rumors with papers evidences that Joe M. was dumped and it was time for Joe T to enjoy Irene's love, I couldn't believe that everybody was laughing at me, I never experienced that kind of shame before, that was way too much that I wanted to redeem myself from that world.

I decided to part ways with Irene for good to redeem myself my shame and avery sort of mocks I was receiving, I wanted to try my life without her. I never rested since the moment I started dating her, I was in an endless fight, always and alot of people hated me because I would take her side in any situation infront of me I was indeed tired that day, even if we had some days lef gor our forecer departure, I could no longer hold on.

I told Irene all that I was tjinking and she should never pretend to be sait-like person, instead she should live her life like she always wanted, I told her that I never wanted to be the obstacle and I'm out of her.

She tried to beg forgiveness several times without getting tired but my 'no was never yes' and that was the last time I remember dating Irene.

****I decided to call it off for good though I later on came to realize that Irene was trying to get out of Joe T's hands but I hurried to the conclusion and she was waiting for me to help her out of those troubles but I was only watching her moves alm in all the story ended in a very regretful way.

Lonely Forever After

When I came to MHDSTR, all I wanted to do was to make my life from there, I cared none from the opposite sex or any sort of feelings towards them. Ally, a friend of mine showed me a way to girls that's when I met Marry and I had a starting point to the life I feared the most, when I became an expert to girls I went on tasting every meal infront of me without looking or considering its preparations. Later on I met a girl whom I hated the most at MHDSTR, she was called Irene, a very beautiful and the brightest of all girls whom was made up by full of ego because she knew she was beautiful, an Andromeda who every man wished to date. She Introduced me in the world I never reached, The World of Love and Romance. Then, she escaped and left me alone to always be lonely.

I though It would be easier to live without her because I didn't notice if I ever missed or loved her that much though I knew that I loved and missed her but I though I would move on with my life even without her, and guess what happened! Only cries would cool me down, I missed her alot and I knew that I never loved someone as much as I loved her.

****

Lonely had taken me into another level. I broke up with Irene and we were hundreds of kilometers away from each other while I was inches away from missing her. I fought all the thought that woukd suggest that I will never see Irene again, I hoped I will settle things and I surely will meet her, but That was never the true case. I happened to talk to her several times but we never made up, she denied me all the times and didn't request from the heart, I knew that I had started giving up on her and I no longer need her as an essential part of me.

Out of frustration and hoping that I would find Irene's replacement, I went on dating dozens of girls, cheated and played in them but none came, It reached a time qhen I forced myself to love but the more I forced myself, the more I hated that person and I ended being a good playboy but after five years, I found another one whom I loved and cared, whenever I look into Irene's pictures I realize thay, I'm no longer her's, That God I moved on from this Andromeda I feared, IRENE.

But, all I could think in my heart was that, Irene never loved me, she never missed me and I was nothing to her as what she always showed me but one time I talked to her concerning the abortion she had done which would take off her entire career because she nearly dropped from high school because of abortion, at that time I was neither even dating her nor having close relationship with her, she threw all the blames on me that I nearly spoiled her life like that and I wanted to know how because I never even saw her three years had passed, she said that I had craved a big skull on her heart and I was so selfish dumping her, she said that she went on dating on anyone seducing her to find my replacement but she failed as I did and pregnant was all she got, and that's when she tried to abort it, a decision that nearly costed her life but she succeeded.

END

www.ingramcontent.com/pod-product-compliance
Lightning Source LLC
LaVergne TN
LVHW041753190726
843493LV00008B/2605